Steven Evans

THE
Library
FOUNDATION

Enhancing the work of our library
libraryfoundation.org

To William

First U.S. edition 2015

Library of Congress Catalog Card Number 2013957523
ISBN 978-0-7636-7480-9

SCP 20 19 18 17 16 15
10 9 8 7 6 5 4 3 2 1

Printed in Humen, Dongguan, China

This book was typeset in Little Grog.
The illustrations were done in mixed media.

Candlewick Press
99 Dover Street
Somerville, Massachusetts 02144

visit us at www.candlewick.com

The *Fly*

Petr Horáček

CANDLEWICK PRESS

Two googly eyes,
six hairy legs,
two transparent wings . . .

It's ME!
The housefly.
But people don't like me
being in the house.

After breakfast, I do my exercises—156 times around

the lamp keeps me fit.

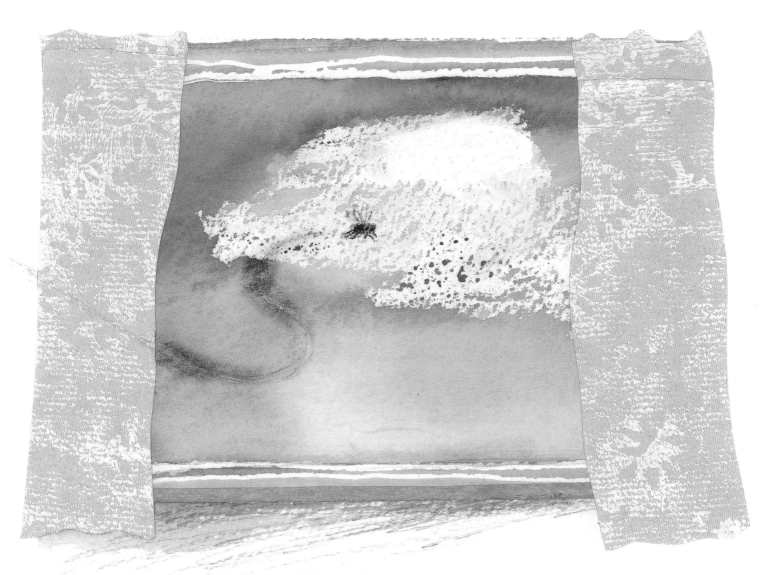

Then it's time for a snack.
I don't mind sharing, but he
doesn't want to share with me.
Flap! That was close!

I think they smell lovely.

But the animals don't really like me. I don't know why.

Once a frog nearly ate me,

then a bird nearly caught me.

Both in the same day.
Why?

I go back to the house for lunch.
I like my meals on time!

I can never understand

FLAP!

FLAP!

FLAP! what all the fuss is about. **FLAP!**

Even when I find a good place to rest . . .

into trouble.

As you can see,
my life is not an easy one.
I'm just a simple creature.
I mean no harm to anyone.
So, if you see me, please be kind.

HEY, don't close the book. . . .

HELP . . . HELP . . .
Do you want to
squash me?